THE UNLUCKY WOMAN

JONATHAN DUNSKY

The Unlucky Woman

Jonathan Dunsky

Copyright © 2018 by Jonathan Dunsky

Cover by OliviaProDesign

Cover photographs © Gladkov/DepositPhotos (Man); joachimbago.gmail.-com/DepositPhotos (Street); laurenthive/DepositPhotos (fog)

ISBN: 9781731028983

Visit JonathanDunsky.com for news and information.

BOOKS BY JONATHAN DUNSKY

ADAM LAPID SERIES

Ten Years Gone

The Dead Sister

The Auschwitz Violinist

A Debt of Death

A Deadly Act

The Auschwitz Detective

A Death in Jerusalem

The Unlucky Woman (short story)

STANDALONE NOVELS

The Payback Girl

1

She was a small woman, fair of complexion and dark of hair, with large brown eyes in which sadness and distress shone gloomily.

An hour earlier, while I was drinking coffee at Greta's Café, a boy of eight had come to my table with a letter from her.

"This is for you," he said with the seriousness of a man a score of years older. "I'm supposed to wait for your answer."

Inside the plain envelope was a note. On it, in a neat and careful hand, was written a short message:

Dear Mr. Lapid,

I have need of a detective. It is a matter of some urgency. I hope that you are free.

Unfortunately, I am unable to come to you. Will you be so kind as to drop by my apartment on Hanevi'im Street at your earliest convenience? Please give Dan your reply.

Thank you,

Hilda Lipkind

It was a balmy autumn day, and I had little to do, so I told Dan to tell Hilda Lipkind that I would be there within the hour. He nodded solemnly, recited the precise address, and hurried off to give her the news. I folded the note and put it in my pocket, finished my coffee and the chess game I'd been playing, and bid Greta goodbye. Then I walked uptown to Hanevi'im Street, where I located Hilda Lipkind's building, climbed the stairs to her third-floor apartment, and was shown to a chair in her modestly appointed living room. She reclined on a ratty old sofa.

Looking at her, I noticed things. Shadows under her eyes. Worry lines at the corners of her mouth. A slumped posture of despair and fatigue. A simple wedding band, which she kept fiddling with. And, of course, a prominent bulge in her abdomen.

Some women in her condition look radiant. She, on the other hand, gave the impression of a weakening light bulb flickering its last light before burning out.

One of those, I thought moodily, half wishing she had not sought me out. The kind of job she would likely offer me was not one that I liked. It was the sort of job that could bring my client nothing but further misery, along with a heart-wrenching truth. Still, I was in no position to decline job offers. They did not come that often, and I needed the money.

I supposed her pregnancy was what had prevented her from coming to see me, but I didn't ask.

"Thank you for coming, Mr. Lapid," Hilda Lipkind said. Her Hebrew was tinged with a distinct Silesian accent. She had grown up somewhere in the eastern parts of Germany, on land that was now either within the new borders of Poland or those of the German Democratic Republic, where not a hint of democracy could be found.

"It's no trouble, Mrs. Lipkind. What can I do for you?"

She hesitated. Some clients are like that. They know they're in trouble. They want my help. But a part of them clings to the belief that things are, in fact, not as bad as they seem, that if they just leave well enough alone, all will be well again. The moment they hire me, that belief turns to dust.

For some obscure reason—her being pregnant and so obviously distressed, perhaps—I decided to ease her into it. Gesturing at her stomach, I said, "When are you due?"

"In two months. December."

"Congratulations."

"Thank you," she said, her tone as flat as a tombstone, as dead as what lay beneath one.

"Your first?"

A dark cloud swept over her anguished face. She placed both hands on her abdomen as though to protect the child within from some threat.

"Yes. I—" She paused, unsure whether to put her thoughts into words. Then she said, "Yes, this will be our first."

She did not smile when she said this, and her frown made it clear my question had brought with it a measure of pain.

"What are you hoping for? A boy or a girl?"

She gave a shrug of helplessness, hopelessness, of utter unhappiness.

Yes, I thought. *Definitely one of those.*

"And your husband? What does he want?"

Her eyes welled with tears, and she brought out a handkerchief and put it to good use.

"A girl. My husband says he wants a girl. Maybe that's true, but I can't tell for certain. Not anymore."

"Why is that?"

"Because these days I don't know when my husband is being truthful and when he isn't. And if he lies about some things, why not about others?"

Her logic was unimpeachable and the sort that could do her very little good.

A flush rose in her cheeks. "Perhaps I was wrong to ask you to come here. I feel bad simply doubting him, as though I'm tarnishing his name."

I remained silent, giving her the chance to ask me to leave. When she didn't, I said, "But you doubt him nonetheless."

She let out a sigh. "I'm afraid so. I try not to, but I can't convince myself that everything he tells me is the truth."

"What is it you think he's hiding?"

"Another woman, I suppose."

"You think he's having an affair? Why?"

"Every evening, after he comes home and the two of us have dinner together, he goes out and does not return until well past ten at night."

"How long has this been going on?"

"A week. A miserable week."

"Where does he go?"

"He says he has to work late, that there's this big project at work, and that if he finishes it quickly, he might get a promotion and a raise. He says we could use the extra money with a new baby on the way. But when I ask him what this project is, he says he can't talk about it yet, that it's confidential. He even went out last Friday. Who works on a Friday evening? Does this make sense to you?"

It did not, but I refrained from telling her that. "What does he do for a living?"

"He's a clerk. He works for the city."

"And he can't support a wife and a child on his salary?"

"Other people do, so why can't he? Sure, we have to make do with little, but everyone else manages. I told him that the third night he went out, begged him to stay with me, but he simply said he had to work. He wouldn't meet my eyes when he said this. He used to love spending the evening with me. Now I have to stay up late just to see him before I turn in."

"Does he have a telephone in his office?"

"Yes."

"Have you tried calling him during the evening when he claims to be working?"

She shook her head. "We don't have a telephone in the apartment. No one in the building does. In normal times, I would walk down to a nearby café and call from there, but these days, even that minor exertion is forbidden me."

Seeing my raised eyebrow, she explained, "You asked before if this was our first child, and I said that it was. But it's not the first time I've been pregnant. It's the fourth. I've had three miscarriages, Mr. Lapid. Two girls and a boy. So the doctor has ordered me to avoid any physical effort, to stay off my feet, and to rest as much as possible. This is why I couldn't come to see you, but had to send Dan with the letter."

"I see," I told her, reading on her face a clear preference to not be consoled over the loss of her three children. I could understand that. She must have gotten a surfeit of commiseration over the years, and I knew from experience how little good that usually did.

"You could ask a neighbor to call on your behalf, couldn't you?"

"I could, but that would invite questions. Suppose I'm wrong and my husband answered the call—what would the neighbor have said? And if he didn't, what would that prove? He might have been momentarily out of the office when the phone rang. The only way for me to prove he's lying is either to call several times—something which I would not ask any neighbor to do—or send someone to check on him. Either way, it would have become public knowledge that we were having problems. I would rather keep this matter private, Mr. Lapid."

I nodded, appreciating the delicacy of her predicament. She was unable to verify her husband's veracity on her own, and she dared not enlist a neighbor or acquaintance to do so on her behalf. And so she turned to me.

Again I wished she had never approached me. But now that she had, and after seeing the anguish etched on her face, I knew there was no escaping it. I would take on her assignment and see it through to its likely bitter end.

"So you want me to find out what your husband does and who he sees?"

Hilda Lipkind nodded, making an observable effort to maintain her composure. She still clutched the handkerchief in one hand, but her eyes were dry. She was a strong woman. Stronger than she looked. "I would like to know if my husband is having an affair, and if so, with whom."

2

We talked next about money. It was clear by her clothes and the furnishing of the apartment that she did not have much. On the other hand, it would likely be a simple job and not one that would take very long.

I named a price that was far from high. Still, it must have stung, as I saw her jaw muscles tighten. But she did not haggle, just heaved herself laboriously off the sofa and shuffled over to a small dining table on which her purse sat. From it she extracted a five-lira note and some coins and handed them to me.

I put them in my pocket, got out my notebook and pencil, and flipped to an empty page.

"I need some information," I said. "Your husband's name for starters. And I need to know what he looks like. Do you have a current picture?"

She told me his name was David and pointed to a shelf on which three framed pictures stood. "The one on the left is the most recent."

I went over and took a look. He was a handsome man, with a full head of wavy black hair and a broad, open face with strong features. His nose was straight and his chin had a deep notch. It was the sort of face most people would describe as honest, but I had learned long ago to discount such impressions. I had suffered at the hands of mild-featured monsters and had received compassion and mercy from brutish saints.

I committed his countenance to memory. I had no doubt I would recognize him easily wherever I chanced on him.

I returned to my chair and said, "You told me your husband goes out each evening. Is it always at the same time?"

"Just about. Around seven, give or take a few minutes. And he is anxious to go. I can tell by the way he wolfs down his dinner." Her voice had taken on a keen edge of insult and pain.

"Does he change his clothes? Take a shower?"

"No, he doesn't," she said thoughtfully. Her expression brightened a little. "He would do that, wouldn't he, if he was going to meet a woman?"

Or he might be smart enough to know that would be a dead giveaway. But I kept that thought to myself.

"I wouldn't jump to conclusions either way, Mrs. Lipkind."

Her face reacquired its dejected cast. "No. I suppose you're right."

"What does he do when he comes home from wherever it is he goes to? Does he head for the shower straightaway?"

"As soon as he comes through the door."

Which didn't have to mean anything either. But it might indicate a desire to wash the scent of a lover off his skin before his wife could detect it.

"How about his clothes? Have you ever caught the smell of perfume on them? Something you yourself do not use. Or a smudge of makeup on his collar?"

She shook her head. "There was nothing like that. But more often than not, his breath smelled of alcohol."

"Is that unusual? He doesn't drink?"

"Not often. And when he does, it's never a lot. These past days, though, it's more than usual. I can tell by his eyes and the slow way he talks that he's had too much. Just how much changes from day to day."

"Did you ask him about it?"

"Once. He snapped at me, told me he was entitled to have a glass of wine from time to time. Then he looked ashamed of losing his temper."

"And is this also unusual, or does he have a short fuse?"

"No. He's very gentle. He hardly ever raises his voice. This is..." She lowered her gaze to her hands and shook her head. "This is terrible. I can't believe this is happening." She raised her eyes to me. They glistened. "We've been married for five years, Mr. Lapid, and in all that time I have never once suspected my husband was not completely devoted to me. I feel guilty doubting him, but I can't help what I think and what I fear. Do you understand?"

"Where did you meet?" I asked.

"In a refugee camp near Hamburg. November 1945. Neither of us had any family left. David's parents, sister, and two brothers were all murdered by the Nazis. My mother died shortly before the war, and my father killed himself in 1940 from despair. He couldn't stand being a Jew in Germany. I was their only child. After the war, David and I were both alone in the world. In January 1946, we married and became a family of two. I got pregnant the first time almost immediately, and when I was four months along, I miscarried."

She paused, obviously pained by the memory. Then she said, "We boarded a ship together, hoping to immigrate to Mandatory Palestine, but the British deported the lot of us to Cyprus. Which is where I had my second miscarriage. Eventually, in October 1948, we were released and arrived in Haifa. I got pregnant again, and this time managed to carry the child for six months. We moved here seven months ago. I must have gotten pregnant our first week here." Her hands tightened atop her ballooning belly, and her eyes locked on mine. She tilted her chin upward in an expression of determination and defiance. "I've never made it this long, Mr. Lapid. In two months, I will give birth to my first child. To our first child. I need to know if my husband is faithful to me. Please, find out the truth."

3

It was a quarter to seven that evening when I returned to Hanevi'im Street. Earlier that day, Hilda Lipkind had told me she watched her husband from the window of their apartment whenever he went out and that he invariably walked westward. So I took up position across the street and a few buildings to the east of theirs. There I waited for David Lipkind to appear.

He did so at three minutes past seven. He strode out of his building with his hands thrust into the pockets of his trousers and his head turned a bit downward. As his wife had said, he began walking to the west. He did not look my way once.

I gave him some space and followed from the opposite sidewalk. I kept my eyes pointed forward, so if he chose to glance over his shoulder at me, it would not appear that I was in any way interested in him.

His gait was determined, his step quick, like a man on a mission. Watching him, I sensed a tension in his back and shoulders, but it might have been nothing but an illusion caused by the fact that his hands were still lodged in his pockets.

At the corner of Hanevi'im and King George, he took a left and disappeared from view. I wasn't worried. I was less than ten seconds behind. I wouldn't lose him.

I realized my mistake as soon as I got to the same corner and made the same turn.

For when I did, I saw David Lipkind boarding a bus two dozen meters to the south. There was no one behind him.

I had a decision to make and but a fraction of a second in which to make it. I could shout for the driver to wait and run to catch the bus before it left the station. But if I did, I would attract attention. Lipkind might take note of my face. Perhaps it would make but a fleeting impression on him, but there was a chance he'd remember me. And if he happened to see me again, it might make him suspicious.

I did not shout or run. The doors of the bus swung shut. Its engine coughed as the driver put it into gear. I watched it rattle its way down King George Street with my quarry on board. I noted the bus number, knowing it would do me little good. That particular line had many stops, and there was no way to tell at which Lipkind would disembark or where he would go once he did.

Swearing softly, I rummaged in my pocket for my cigarettes. I stuck one between my lips and puffed away at it, feeling that I had failed my client and vowing that tomorrow would be different.

4

A little before seven the next evening, I waited for Lipkind again. But this time I chose a different location. Instead of on his street, where I could see his building, I stood a few doors down from the bus stop where I'd lost him the previous day.

I was taking a risk, but it was a calculated one. My client had told me her husband always walked westward when he went on one of his evening trips. I was betting he boarded the same bus each time, and today I planned to be on it.

My confidence gradually waned as the minutes dragged by, and when my wristwatch showed a quarter past seven, I began to believe I had made a mistake. Perhaps Lipkind had chosen that evening to change his route, or maybe he hadn't gone out at all.

At seven twenty-five I was ready to call it a night. I tossed what remained of my cigarette into the gutter and was about to turn south toward home, when he finally appeared.

He wore black pants and a blue buttoned shirt. This time, only his left hand was wedged in his pocket; the right was swinging loosely at his side.

He halted at the bus stop, extracted his left hand, and glanced at his wristwatch. His lips pulled back from his teeth, and he muttered something I didn't catch. Some curse word, probably.

Tapping his foot, he gazed north to where the bus would be coming from. I kept my eyes averted, so I could only see him at the edges of my vision. There were two other persons at the stop, one man and one woman. Neither of them approached Lipkind, nor did anyone else.

I lit a cigarette, feeling relieved. I had not made a mistake. I was at the right place at the right time.

Ten minutes passed before the bus arrived. During that time, Lipkind's agitation grew dramatically. He began pacing and running his lower lip back and forth between his teeth. He must have checked the time once a minute if not more. Wherever he was going, he was in a hurry to get there. No man was that anxious to get to his office, no matter how important his job was. Hilda Lipkind was right. He was hiding something. Tonight I would find out what—or who—it was.

When the bus pulled into the station, I hung back, allowing Lipkind and the other two to board ahead of me. The smell of a dozen cigarette brands hung thickly in the interior of the bus. I paid my fare and found a seat at the back. Lipkind chose a seat next to the rear doors. I turned my head away from him as I walked past his seat, but it seemed an unnecessary precaution. He was gazing out the window, and the look in his eyes suggested that he was not staring at anything in particular.

I lit another cigarette and kept my eyes on the back of Lipkind's head as the bus wound its way down King George. We passed Gan Meir Park and the corner of Hamaccabi Street where I lived. Lipkind did not move.

The bus turned left onto Allenby Street, passed Greta's Café and the corner of Balfour Street, and then slowed and coasted to a stop. Lipkind shot up from his seat as though launched by a coiled spring and was at the rear door before the bus had come to a complete stop. I disembarked third after a heavyset middle-aged woman carrying a hefty purse.

Out on the street, Lipkind began marching north, and for a second I was certain his destination was Greta's Café. It was highly unlikely because I had spent more than one evening there over the past week and had seen no sign of him. I let him build a lead and followed.

He did not go to Greta's. Instead, he turned right onto Balfour Street. I paused at the corner and watched him stride purposefully to an imposing building I knew well. The Hadassah Hospital, where I had been hospitalized after taking two bullets in Israel's War of Independence.

He entered the front courtyard and disappeared behind the stone fence. I hurried after him, perplexed. I had expected him to go to a café or restaurant or the apartment of a lover. A hospital did not strike me as a suitable location for a tryst.

Then again, maybe his paramour was a nurse. Maybe she was married, too. A hospital offered plenty of secluded spots, and one could always find a vacant bed, cot, or mattress if one knew where to look.

I went through the metal gate, walking quickly now, past two nurses who sat on a bench smoking and chatting, and got to the front doors five seconds after Lipkind. He did not stop in the lobby but headed straight for the stairs and started taking them two at a time. He was nearly running now, and just like the previous night, I could not afford to do the same for fear of drawing attention to myself.

Instead, I crossed the lobby and climbed the stairs at a pace just a shade faster than normal, losing sight of him around the bend in the staircase and knowing that there was a risk I would not be able to locate him that night. The hospital was a large building, and there were places in it I would not be able to scour for him.

At the second floor, I looked to both sides but did not see him. The air was redolent of that astringent clean smell common to hospitals. A chill shivered up my spine as I recalled my own time in the hospital, the pain of injury and recovery. I shook away the memory and resumed the search. I prowled the hallway, peered into open doorways, and even checked the public lavatory. No sign of Lipkind.

There were rooms I did not check, those with closed doors or ones clearly reserved for the use of staff. It was an imperfect search, to be sure, but with hospital staff constantly roving about, it was the best I could do.

Finally, I returned to the stairs, ascended to the third floor, and repeated my search.

I found Lipkind two doors from the eastern end of the hallway.

5

It was a small austere room with a single bed, and David Lipkind was sitting at the side of it. On the bed lay a woman covered by a white blanket from the neck down. From my vantage point, peeking around the edge of the doorway, I could only catch a partial view of her. I saw that her eyes were closed, her skin was pale, and her black hair had been cut close to her scalp. A thick bandage encircled her head.

Lipkind sat hunched over, elbows on knees, his forehead resting on his clasped hands. A slight tremor vibrated across his shoulders and upper back. With his head lowered and his back almost fully to me, I could not see his face, but his mood was unmistakable. This wasn't a man bubbling with sexual excitement at the prospect of meeting an illicit lover. This was a man whose soul was in agony.

As I stood there watching, he began mumbling, his voice barely carrying to where I stood. I caught snatches of his mono-logue and identified the language as Polish. I had picked up a smattering of the language during my time in Auschwitz, but not nearly enough to understand the majority of what Lipkind was saying.

Against my better judgment, I found myself rooted to the spot, my eyes locked on his anguished form. It was reckless of me; he might turn at any moment and find me staring at him. But I was somehow convinced this would not occur. He appeared completely focused, ensnared by the female patient to whom he was speaking.

Seeing him in this state was strangely fascinating, but after a minute, a sense of unease crept over me. This was a moment that warranted privacy, and I was intruding upon it. After a final glance, I turned away from the room and halfway to the stairs found an alcove with a small table and some chairs, from which I could keep track of the hallway.

I lowered myself into one and wondered what all this meant. Who was the woman in the hospital bed? What was her connection to David Lipkind? And why did he keep her secret from his wife?

On the small table, someone had left a copy of that day's *Haaretz*. I smoked a cigarette while leafing through the paper, trying to steer my thoughts away from these as yet unanswerable questions. I read the paper all the way through and in that time did not see David Lipkind. I smoked a second cigarette and then a third, and still he did not show. Curious, I finally rose and walked back to the room with the sleeping woman.

There he still was, sitting in that same chair. Only now he wasn't mumbling. He was crying instead. His weeping was soft, barely audible, yet it wasn't as restrained as its volume. His shoulders shook with it, as did his head and the hands that covered his face.

Again, I had the sense that I was witnessing something I shouldn't. I returned to the waiting alcove and sat there until a nurse informed me that visiting hours were over and that I ought to leave. It was nine o'clock.

I nodded to her and said that I'd be going. I made my way downstairs to the lobby and there leaned against the back wall and waited. Five minutes later, David Lipkind stepped off the lowermost stair and began crossing the lobby toward the exit. Gone was the purposeful stride. Now he walked slowly, ponderously, as though he wasn't sure where he was going. His handsome face was dry, his expression stony, but there was no mistaking the redness of his eyes.

He stepped out of the lobby and into the night. I counted to ten silently and followed. He headed straight toward the gate and turned left. At the corner he turned left again, plodded past the corner of Maze and Allenby, entered the first café he came across, and found a stool at the bar. One of the four small outdoor tables was vacant. I took it and ordered a coffee. Lipkind opted for something harder. The bartender poured him a glass of red wine, which Lipkind proceeded to drain without delay. The fact that the bartender remained standing nearby with the bottle in his hand told me that Lipkind was a repeat customer who could be counted upon for a refill.

This was confirmed two seconds later when Lipkind set his empty glass on the bar and gave a quick nod to the bartender. He poured him another glass and then wandered off to see to the needs of another patron.

For a long while, Lipkind just sat there with the refilled glass at his elbow. He did not talk to anyone. He seemed absorbed in his own thoughts. Finally, he turned his attention back to the wine and gulped it down as though it were medicine. Then he put some money on the bar, glanced at his wristwatch, shoved his hands in his pockets, and lumbered out.

I followed him with my eyes to the bus station where he could catch the same line as before, only this time in the opposite direction. When the bus arrived a little after ten, I did not board it with him. I was done trailing him for tonight. His wife had told me he came home between ten and eleven. I guessed that was where he was headed now.

I paid for my coffee and made my way north. I passed Greta's Café, but she had already closed for the night. I went home, got into bed, and slept in the company of my dark dreams.

6

The next morning, right after breakfast, I returned to Hadassah Hospital. My goal was to learn the name of the woman David Lipkind had visited the night before and understand his connection to her.

The hospital bustled with activity, and no one paid me any mind as I climbed to the third floor and made my way to the room where the young woman lay.

A strong-bodied nurse was with her. I watched from the doorway as the nurse took her pulse and dabbed her lips with a piece of cloth. Then she moved to the foot of the bed and took hold of one of the patient's legs and began manipulating it—bending and stretching and rotating it methodically, again and again. She repeated this with the other leg and then with each arm.

Throughout this entire process, the woman in the bed did not open her eyes, nor did her expression—what I could see of it—change one bit. She wasn't asleep, I realized, but in a coma.

In the midst of her ministrations, alerted by some mysterious sense, the nurse suddenly stopped and whipped her head around. "Can I help you?"

She was in her late forties, her black hair rolled into a tight bun. Her round face and brown eyes appeared capable of kindness, but at that moment her forehead was furrowed and her eyes narrowed in suspicion.

I put on what I hoped was a disarming smile, but inside I was chiding myself for not working out a credible story in advance. What had I been thinking, that I could simply waltz into this hospital and all the information I needed would fall in my lap? I gestured at the woman in the bed. "My name is Adam Lapid, and I would be grateful if you'd tell me what her condition is."

"Are you a relative of Miss Lipkind?"

I frowned in surprise. Miss Lipkind? This comatose woman was related to David Lipkind?

"No," I said. "I'm not."

"Then why do you want to know how she's doing? Are you with the police?"

For the second time in about twice as many seconds, I felt surprised. Why would the police be interested in this woman? And why would David Lipkind hide her existence from his wife?

I could guess the answer to the first of these two questions. If the police were involved, it was likely that an assault of some kind was the reason this woman was now in a coma.

I gave the nurse a quick appraising look. One of her hands was laid protectively on top of the patient's arm; the other was braced in the crook of her waist. Her tone matched the look in her eyes—wary and mistrustful. I had posed as a policeman several times before—it came easy since I had been one before the World War —but something told me this would not work on this woman.

"May I know your name?" I said, hoping to build some rapport with this nurse and also buy myself some time to come up with a good reason for my presence. The truth, I was fairly certain, would not suffice.

"Meira Golobinski. Now answer my question: why are you here?"

An idea tumbled into my mind like manna from Heaven. "I'm an investigator," I said slowly, tasting the words as they came out, becoming more confident in them with each syllable. "I work for an insurance company. Miss Lipkind had a policy and—"

"You mean has," the nurse said sharply. "She's not dead, as you can see."

I inclined my head. "You're right. I apologize. She *has* a policy. Can you tell me what her condition is?"

The nurse pursed her lips, her eyes probing the length and breadth of my face.

I did not particularly like myself for lying to her, but this case had gone from a simple matter of verifying a husband's infidelity to something far more mysterious. My client had a right to know what was leading her husband to abandon her each evening to come to this woman's bedside. If I had to tell a small lie to provide my client with a great truth, then I would do so. Even if this made me feel the opposite of proud.

Nurse Golobinski considered me for a minute longer, and I became certain she would refuse my request and order me to go away and never return. But then she exhaled loudly and her hand fell from her waist. "Perhaps it is I who owes you an apology, Mr. Lapid. Patients in this condition are the most vulnerable patients we have. There have been incidents—well, I prefer not to get into that."

"Why did you think I was with the police?" I said, knowing the answer but hoping the question would elicit more information from her.

"You have a look about you, that's all. And I keep waiting for a policeman to come and see her. It's outrageous that they can simply close a case without once seeing the victim."

"Oh, is the case closed already?"

"You didn't know? From what I hear, they determined the driver was not responsible, that it was actually her fault." Her voice rang with indignation. "Can you grasp that? Because I can't. She gets hit by a car and goes into a coma and it's somehow her fault? How can this be? What are the police thinking?"

I shrugged and, latching onto what I'd just learned from her, said, "I don't know the particulars of the case, I'm afraid. Only that she was struck by a vehicle."

"Well, if you ask me, they should put the driver in a dank cell somewhere until she comes out of it." She paused and turned her eyes toward the comatose woman. The indignation melted off her face, replaced by sorrowful compassion. She sighed and looked once more at me. "It's not my place to brief anyone on her condition, Mr. Lapid, but I'll ask Dr. Meles if he'll see you. Come with me. There's a waiting area down the hall. You can wait there."

She ushered me to the same alcove where I'd sat the previous night. "Sit here, Mr. Lapid. Either I or Dr. Meles will be with you shortly." Then she turned away in search of the doctor, her low-heeled shoes clanking a fast rhythm on the floor tiles.

This time there was no newspaper with which to pass the time. It took fifteen minutes and two cigarettes before someone came to see me. Fortunately, it wasn't Nurse Golobinski.

Instead, the man who offered me his hand was tall and spare, with wire-rim glasses and a weak chin. His fringe of sandy hair surrounded a bald scalp to which a handful of forlorn patches of minute hairs clung like seaweed to the hull of a ship. A professional smile creased his weary face.

"I'm Dr. Meles," he said.

I rose and clasped his hand. His grip was dry and not very strong. "Adam Lapid."

"I understand you've been asking about Clara Lipkind, that you work for an insurance company?"

I nodded. "Can you tell me how she's doing?"

We both sat. He removed his glasses and cleaned them with the tail of his white coat. Glassless, his eyes looked watery and weak, which made his face look even more tired than before. I was glad when he put them back on.

"We don't usually share medical information with anyone apart from family members. Or the police if required."

"I understand that, Doctor. But the truth is, I already have the overall picture. It would be very helpful to me, my employers, and to Miss Lipkind and her beneficiaries if you would be willing to share a few extra details."

I waited while he turned the matter over in his mind. Finally he gave a short nod and said, "There isn't much I can add to what's obvious to anyone who's seen her. She's comatose. Has been since she arrived in the hospital."

"She came here right after the accident?"

"Yes. The ambulance brought her straight here. She was unconscious, nonresponsive. At first we were positive she would die that day, but her condition has stabilized to the sorry state she's in now."

"Any other injuries?"

"Some scrapes and abrasions. Nothing more serious than that. It appears that the only severe blow she suffered was on her head. Terrible luck. It would have been better had she broken all four limbs. This—" he shook his head "—this is much worse."

"Is she in pain?"

"She might be. We don't really know. We also don't know whether she's aware of what goes on around her. I prefer to think that she's not."

"How do you feed her?"

"Enterally," he said and, when he saw my puzzlement, added,

"Via a tube. Truth is, we don't have a lot of experience at this sort of procedure, so we must be doing a suboptimal job at it. We lack the proper equipment and nutritional formulas that exist in America and a few other more prosperous countries. Still, we can probably keep her alive for a while as long as no infection or other complication arises. Exactly how long? That's a question neither I nor anyone else can truly answer."

"She's shown no improvement?"

"The day before yesterday she did exhibit some facial activity, mostly around the eyes. This leads us to suppose—to hope—that her mind is still intact and that she may regain consciousness."

"Do you believe she will?"

He spread his hands, and I noticed he had long, thin fingers. "One can never tell in such cases. What we don't know about comas far exceeds what we do know. She might die tomorrow, or she might stay in this exact same state for weeks and then emerge from it. Her chances are not good. They never are with such an injury. What sort of policy does she have with your company?"

I raised an eyebrow. "Are you asking whether we'd prefer her to live or die?"

He cleared his throat. "I did not mean to imply that—"

"I'm sure you didn't, Dr. Meles," I said and, before he had the chance to raise the question of the policy again, continued, "We've been looking for the next of kin. Has she had any visitors, by any chance?"

"Just her brother."

"Brother?"

"Yes. He comes here every evening."

"David Lipkind?"

"Yes. You've spoken to him?"

"No. Not yet," I said absently, digesting this new bit of information and remembering that Hilda Lipkind had told me her husband had lost all his family, including his sister, in the Holocaust.

She might have gotten it wrong, or maybe he had. Every once in a while, a story like that made its way to you, like a candle of hope in a starless night of misery. People who'd lost contact during the war and were sure the other was dead, and then, one day, quite unexpectedly, ran into each other.

Could David Lipkind simply have run into a sister he had been certain was dead? Possible, but it wouldn't explain why he was keeping her a secret from his wife.

There had to be a reason for that. A damn good one.

But what could it be?

And then it struck me that Dr. Meles and the rest of the hospital staff would have no way of knowing whether David Lipkind was indeed Clara Lipkind's brother. But if he wasn't her brother, what was his connection to her?

A theory began forming at the edges of my mind. Unlikely, to be sure, but one that fit. Could it be?

The answer to this question was yes, but I would need to do more digging to find out one way or the other.

"Thank you, Dr. Meles," I said. "You've been most helpful. I appreciate it."

His thin lips formed a satisfied little smile. "Glad to help." He smoothed the lapel of his coat and began to rise. "If you'll excuse me, I need to—"

"Just one more thing. I'd like to see her."

The doctor's eyebrows rose an inch. He checked his watch, rubbing a forefinger across his lips. "All right, but only for a minute, Mr. Lapid."

He turned and began walking briskly toward her room. I followed. Together we entered and stepped close to the bed. I looked down at the motionless woman and knew immediately who she was.

7

"She's his sister," I said.

Hilda Lipkind looked baffled. We were in her living room, two hours after I had left the hospital. I had just given her a short summary of my investigation, culminating in the visit I'd paid to Clara Lipkind's room. Hilda was sitting on her old sofa. Her face and body were tense as though she expected a powerful blow to land upon her at any second but wasn't sure where it would come from. Her hands lay across her distended belly, protecting what was most important to her. "His sister?"

I nodded.

"His sister is dead."

"Apparently not."

"David told me she died."

"He may have thought she did," I said, and explained what I believed had happened: that David and Clara Lipkind were separated during the war, assumed the other was dead, and were just recently reunited. "His sister's name is Clara, isn't it?"

She gave a slow nod, struggling with disbelief and doubt. "Are you absolutely sure that's who this woman is?"

"Beyond a doubt. And if you saw her, you'd have no doubt either. The resemblance between her and your husband is remarkable. Her face is a feminine version of his. Are they twins, by any chance?"

"No. She was two years younger than him. That's almost all I know about her. David doesn't talk much about his family. It's too painful, I think. Or maybe he has another reason. I'm not sure what to think anymore. How did they meet again? Where?"

I told her I didn't know.

"Why didn't he tell me about her? Why the secrets? Why the lies?"

I admitted to not knowing that either. "But he's not seeing a lover. That I can tell you."

She absorbed this bit of news. But if having her worst fears come to naught gave her any joy whatsoever, she exhibited no sign of it.

It was understandable. Learning that her husband was having an affair would have been devastating, but it was also normal, something she could wrap her mind around and begin to deal with. Discovering her husband had a sister he was hiding from her, that he was visiting said sister each evening in the hospital, was not in the least bit normal. It was strange. It demanded an explanation.

We sat in mutual silence for a long moment, and I watched emotions ripple across her face as she struggled to make sense of what her husband was doing.

At length, I reached into my pocket, took out half of the money she'd given me, and laid it on the table between us. That caught her attention.

"What's this?" she asked.

"Half of the retainer you paid me. I've only been at it a couple of days. Half is sufficient payment for my work."

She looked at the money lying there on the table. She did not move to pick it up. She gnawed her lip for a while and then said, "Why do you think he hasn't told me about her?"

"I don't know. You could ask him."

"But then he'd know I'd had him followed, wouldn't he? Otherwise, how could I know he was going to the hospital?"

"You could make something up. Say you heard about it from a neighbor or an acquaintance who spotted him there."

Her mouth curled into a bitter smile. "More lies. More falsehoods. My marriage has enough of those, don't you think? And besides, that wouldn't explain how I know it's his sister." Sighing, she rubbed her face with her hands. "No. I don't want to lie to David. Not even when it's clear he's been lying to me." She looked at me squarely. "Can you imagine what he may be hiding?"

I shook my head. "No idea, I'm afraid."

Using the tips of her fingers, she tapped a quick rhythm against her belly, looking thoughtful. Then she stopped, and I knew she had come to a decision.

"Pick up your money, Mr. Lapid. There's one more thing I'd like you to do for me. I want you to find out why my husband has not told me about all of this."

I looked at her. At this woman with a baby in her belly, love in her heart, and fear in her mind. Her expression was tired and worried, yet steeled with determination. I felt a sudden urge to turn her down, to tell her I was done. I felt like telling her to let this matter go, that she might end up worse off if she didn't.

Yet I knew she wouldn't let it go. And I also found myself curious. I wanted to know what was going on, too. Perhaps if I'd had another case, some other mystery to occupy my time and mind, I'd have felt differently. But I had nothing else, only the mundaneness of everyday life, when my brain was often filled with thoughts and memories that brought me nothing but pain.

So I picked up the money and put it in my pocket.

"All right," I said. "I'll see what I can do."

8

Reuben Tzanani handed me the police report. It consisted of six pages. One of them was typed, the rest handwritten in pencil. "You can read it here if you like, Adam. I doubt it would take you very long."

I nodded and read the report while sitting before his desk at the police station on Yehuda Halevi Street. He, in the meantime, filed away a small mountain of papers in two metal filing cabinets that stood against one wall of his tiny office.

He had the window open, and the city provided a lively sound-track to my reading. It took me fifteen minutes to read the report twice, jotting some notes in my notebook as I went along.

All told, it wasn't much. A routine report about a car accident. Time, place, the names of the driver and the woman who was injured. Baruch Elron was the driver. Clara Lipkind was the victim.

The report contained interviews with witnesses to the accident. Four people in total, all women, gave their descriptions of what had happened. Based on these, the conclusion arrived at by the reporting officer and later approved by his lieutenant was that the driver was not to blame. Reading the interviews, I could not fault their decision. Nurse Golobinski would not have been pleased with me.

After thanking Reuben and giving a vague promise to drop by and visit him and his family in the very near future, I left the police station and made my way north to Sirkin Street. Baruch Elron lived there.

He wasn't in. His wife told me I should look for him at a nearby café. I went over there and found him sitting alone at a table near the rear. A cup of coffee and a plate dotted with crumbs sat on his table next to a batch of newspapers. He was reading *Kol Ha'am*, the paper of the Israeli communist party, when I came over and introduced myself.

He was plump and in his forties, with thinning brown hair, a bulbous nose, and pouches under two narrowly spaced eyes. He looked very tired, and his expression was somber. It turned even more so when I explained what I was there to see him about.

"You want to know what happened?" Baruch Elron said, rubbing one rounded cheek with a short-fingered hand. "I must have told that story a hundred times since it happened. And I've run it through my mind ten thousand times at least. I suppose talking about it again won't hurt. Besides, it's not like I have anything better to do."

He gestured for me to sit and flicked a final glance at the newspaper in his hand before crumpling it and tossing it on a nearby chair. "First time I ever read that rag. I'm the farthest thing from a communist there is, but it's better than sitting around going crazy, you know?"

"Because of the accident?" I said.

"Because of the accident. I can't think of much else since it happened. The sound of the impact, how she flew through the air, seeing her lying there on the pavement with blood gushing from her head. Terrible. Just terrible. Has her condition improved, do you know?"

The look he was giving me was so hopeful, I felt bad for having to tell him the truth.

"Afraid not. She's still in a coma."

His face fell to an even lower depth than before. He looked down at his hands. "It wasn't my fault. Everyone says that. The police, the people who saw it happen, my wife. I know they're right. In my head I know they're right. But I still can't stop thinking I might have done something to prevent it, do you understand?"

He raised his eyes and I could see the pain on his face. He was bottling some of it up inside, as men often do, but all the same it was plain to see. The cast of his features was that of a man tormented.

"Tell me about the accident," I said.

He sniffled a little and cleared his throat. "I'm a taxi driver. I'd just let off a fare near the corner of Frishman and Hayarkon and was driving south looking for another customer. I wasn't going fast, I wasn't distracted. Then, out of nowhere, a woman sprinted from behind a parked car and into the road. I didn't see her until she was right in front of me. I stomped on the brakes and yanked on the wheel, but it was too late. I hit her." He closed his eyes and swallowed hard. "She flew off the hood and onto the road, landing with a thud I could feel in my bones. It was terrible."

"You tried helping her?"

"Of course. I stopped the car and ran to her. She just lay there, motionless. I wiped the blood from her forehead with my handkerchief. Her eyes were closed. I thought she was dead, was sure of it, but a man who'd gotten to her before I did checked her pulse and began shouting that she was alive, that someone should call an ambulance."

I leaned forward, frowning, recalling that all four witnesses were female. "A man? What man?"

"I never asked his name. As you can imagine, I was pretty distraught. I remember I was babbling quite a bit, saying how I didn't see her, how she just ran into the road, and so on and so forth. He didn't seem to notice I was there. He was clutching the woman's hand, talking to her in some foreign language, crying like a child. He looked like he was in shock. Probably, I looked much the same." He fell silent, taking a quick gulp from his cup.

"He wasn't mentioned in the police report," I said. "Any idea why?"

"Yeah. He must have seen the whole thing, but he disappeared right after the ambulance arrived and took her away, even though I pleaded with everyone present to wait for the police." He shrugged. "In the end it didn't matter. Other people told the officers what they saw. I was exonerated. They even gave me my license back. Told me I could go back to driving my taxi any time I wanted. Of course, the car was damaged, but it's been fixed for three days and I still haven't driven it. I'm not sure I want to. I'm scared to get behind the wheel. I'll have to eventually. I have to make a living, you know. But right now, I just can't see myself ever driving again, you understand?"

"This man, he was with the injured woman?"

"No. He came from the opposite sidewalk."

"Can you describe him?"

Elron squinted in concentration as he peered inward into his memory. "Black hair. Late twenties or early thirties. Not too thin, but not fat either. I don't know what else I can tell you. Like I said, I was distraught. I didn't try to remember his face. I was focused on the girl."

"Did he have a notch in his chin?"

Elron stared at me. "You know him? You know who he is?"

I did. It was David Lipkind.

9

I thought I had most of it figured out now. The war in Europe had torn David Lipkind apart from his sister, Clara. Each thought the other had died. Each went about the business of rebuilding their life as best they could after the calamity that had befallen them.

They might easily have passed their remaining years oblivious of the other's continued existence, but fate had brought the two of them to Israel. And on one fateful autumn day in Tel Aviv, it had drawn them to the same street at the same time.

That might not have been enough. They might still have missed each other. And perhaps David did. Perhaps his eyes had wandered to a shopping window or a crack in the sidewalk on which he was stepping. Perhaps he had not been aware that his sister was across the street.

Until she had seen him.

And then the accident happened.

How it happened was now clear to me. Clara Lipkind, seeing her thought-to-be-dead brother on the other side of the street, threw caution to the wind and ran headlong into the road. In that moment of shock and sublime joy, she must have been blind to everything else. Including Baruch Elron's taxi.

She had one thought on her mind, one irresistible desire—to throw her arms around her brother's neck, to hug him long and tight. Or perhaps it was something even more basic than that. Perhaps she simply had to know that it was really him, that he was not some phantom or a figment of her tortured imagination. And the only way to do that was to see him up close, to touch him.

And so she ran without looking. Straight into the path of the taxi.

Had she shouted David's name when she took that first frantic stride? Had he seen her an instant before she was struck? Was that how he'd gotten to her before anyone else?

It was possible, I supposed, but it mattered little. What did matter was that David Lipkind did not tell his wife about any of this. Instead, he lied to her each evening when he went to the hospital to sit at Clara's bedside, to weep over her in solitude.

Why did he do it? Why did he lie? Was it because of guilt? Did he feel responsible for his sister's accident? He had no cause to be; it was just bad luck. But when did logic ever stop anyone feeling guilty or ashamed?

The more I thought about it, though, the more it seemed to me that this wasn't the answer. There had to be another reason for David Lipkind's behavior.

It was my job to find out what it was.

10

The police report said that Clara Lipkind lived on Hahashmal Street and that she had a roommate. I took a bus to Rothschild Boulevard and walked the rest of the way. I found the building without trouble. It wasn't much to look at. A block of old, dirty stone without a hint of beauty. I climbed the stairs to the third floor and knocked on the door. The roommate was in.

Her name was Dorit Henkin. She was twenty-two or twenty-three. Medium height and build. Shoulder-length reddish-brown hair and green eyes a shade or two darker than mine. They were pretty eyes, but there was a hardness to them.

She opened the door holding a mop in one hand. Leaning on it, she looked me up and down with stark disinterest. Her face was slightly flushed. She blew away a strand of hair that had fallen across her face and asked me what I wanted.

I gave her my name and said that I was a private detective. "I'd like to talk to you about your roommate."

"Clara?"

"Is there another one?"

"No. Just me and her. Only now it's just me, I guess. From what

I hear, I shouldn't be expecting her back." If there had been a trace of concern or sorrow in her voice when she'd said this, I must have missed it. "How is she? Any change?"

"No. She's still comatose."

"Oh," she said with that same lukewarm tone. "Okay. I suppose you can come in. Only I won't be able to offer you anything to drink. I just washed the kitchen floor. I want to let it dry before I go in there."

The living room held too much furniture for its modest size: a bulky sofa that hugged one wall; three chairs, none of them from the same set; a square dining table; and a rug that had been rolled up, probably so Miss Henkin could wash the living room floor. It was the sort of furniture you had when you couldn't afford anything better—or even anything worse.

She propped the mop against the table, wiped her hands on her dress, plopped down on the sofa, and crossed her legs. I took one of the chairs. She said, "Well, what do you want to know? Ask away."

"How long have you and Clara been roommates?"

"Six months. Almost seven."

"You knew each other before?"

"No. Clara lived here before I did. Her previous roommate moved out. Clara posted an ad. I was the first to answer it. Lucky me."

"You don't like the apartment?"

She smiled a humorless smile. It seemed to come natural to her. "It's not the best location, is it? And it's cramped. You should see my room; it's even smaller than the living room. But the rent is cheap, and that's all I can afford right now."

"Are you good friends?" I asked, though I was beginning to suspect the answer.

She snorted. "I wouldn't say that."

"What would you say?"

"I'd say we're roommates, nothing more."

"You don't like her much, do you?"

"That's quite perceptive of you, Mr. Detective."

"Any reason why?"

"She talks too much, for one thing. And always about the most depressing subjects."

"Such as?"

"Her family, for the most part. They're all dead, you know. Died in the camps in Europe."

"And she liked talking about them?" I asked in disbelief. For I was the exact opposite. I did not want to talk about my dead family with anyone. Thinking about them was painful enough. Conjuring them up with words might be too much to bear.

Dorit Henkin nodded. "All the time. She would get into this mood. Her eyes would change, turn distant, and her mouth would sort of droop, and I'd know she was about to launch into one of her boring stories of a time gone by." She cast her voice higher and adopted a mock Polish accent, mimicking, I guessed, Clara Lipkind's manner of speech. It set my teeth on edge. "'How wonderful they were. Mama and Papa. They both worked together in the clothing store. Papa did the tailoring and Mama the selling. They made such beautiful clothes. All the best people would shop there. Even those who weren't fond of Jews.'"

She paused, pretending to wipe away tears. I stared at her in mute disgust. Not only did Dorit Henkin feel no compassion for Clara Lipkind for what she had gone through in Europe, and not only did she not care that Clara was now fighting for her life in the hospital, but she was actually mocking her. Was she simply heart-less? Or did she grow to hate her roommate over time?

She continued, still in that fake, high-pitched voice. "'Later, when things became bad, Papa had to close the store. Mama had to clean houses for money. But she always wore a smile when she was at home. Even when she was tired and worn-out and dejected.

39

She always had that beautiful smile. That beautiful, beautiful smile.'" She made her voice break on those last words, her face crimping as though she were about to cry. Then her expression smoothed out, and she gave me a smirk while reclining on the sofa.

In her regular voice, she said, "I have no idea why she kept telling me about them, again and again, when I wasn't even pretending to look interested."

"Because she had no one else," I said.

She blinked, and for a second or two a frown carved shallow lines across her forehead. Then the frown was gone, and she said, "Anyway, it got tedious listening to the same stories over and over. And she would complain a lot, too. About the heat, the dust, anything you can imagine. It got so bad I made it a point to spend as much time as I could out of the apartment. Anything to not hear her grouse."

Looking at me, she tilted her head slightly and grinned. "Did I shock you? I did, didn't I? You certainly have that look on your face. Well, if I did, it's too bad. You're the one who came here with all your questions. I just answered them. Anything else you want to know? Because I need to get back to my cleaning."

I wanted nothing more than to see the last of her, but I masked my distaste. I needed information she might possess. "What did Clara say about her brother?"

A look of confusion came over Dorit Henkin's face. I liked her better this way. Less cold. "What brother? She had no brother."

"David," I said.

She looked at me as if she found me to be incredibly stupid. Then she burst out laughing. "You're not much of a detective, are you?"

I said nothing. Just waited for her to stop laughing and elaborate. It took nearly a minute.

"David isn't her brother. Though I guess I understand why

you'd think so. He was the subject of her most favorite stories to tell and retell. And the most boring of the lot." She fluttered her lashes and seemed on the verge of launching once more into that high-pitched impression of hers—but I cut her off before she had the chance.

"Stop it! Just tell me what you know."

She flinched. I hadn't meant to, but my voice had come out as a growl. She had not been expecting that. I leaned forward, my eyes welded to hers.

"What's this about David not being Clara's brother? I've seen the man myself—he survived, by the way, lives here in Tel Aviv—if he's not her brother, then I'm—"

"David's alive?" There was genuine wonder in her voice. She no longer looked disinterested.

"Very much so."

An insidious little smile curled her lips, and she let out a low chuckle. "My God," she said. "Of all the bad luck. It turns out he's alive, and Clara gets hit by a car and goes into a coma. It's almost too cruel to happen to anyone, even to her."

"Why do you hate her so much? And don't tell me it's because she told boring stories too often. I know about hate. It's a fire that needs a stronger fuel than that to burn bright and hot."

Dorit Henkin pursed her lips and was silent for a long moment. Then she said, "The way Clara told it, everyone thought she and David were sister and brother. They used to laugh about it, the two of them. They took it as a sign. Some couples grow to resemble one another over the years; they were that way from the very beginning. And not only that, but David even had a sister named Clara! Imagine that." She had aimed for sarcasm when she'd said that last bit, but her tone had sounded bitter. And judging by the way she cleared her throat, she was aware of it.

I sat back, trying to assimilate what I'd just heard. It was incredible, to be sure, but life offers a multitude of improbable moments and incidents. "You mean they were—"

"Husband and wife," she said. "Got married in 1939. Way Clara told it, there has never been a love like theirs in all the history of the world." She rolled her eyes. "First sight, soul mates, meant for each other—you name the cliché, she said it. It got irritating fast."

I shut my eyes and thought of Hilda Lipkind. How would she take this news? Pretty badly, I suspected. And it was up to me to break it to her. Somewhere deep inside, I felt a sharp twinge. A little for myself, but mostly for Hilda.

My eyes still closed, I said, "What happened to them?"

"Same thing that happened to other Jews. David died. At least, that's what Clara thought. You say he lives here in Tel Aviv? I wonder..."

I opened my eyes. "Wonder what?"

"If he is being faithful to her. Clara said that she and David had made a vow to each other. They were to belong to one another till the end of time. If he were to die, she would keep on loving him for the rest of her life. And the same went for him. Because their love could never die, understand? It was so powerful and special and unique that it would be impossible for either of them to fall in love with anyone else. Stupid, eh? It always sounded to me like juvenile romantic nonsense. But Clara took it very seriously. She kept her vow like a nun keeps hers." Dorit Henkin's green eyes flashed with wicked mischief. "So tell me, detective, did David Lipkind keep his vow to Clara? Or was she as big a fool as I thought?"

I gave her a long look and suddenly it came to me. The fuel for the fire of her hatred. "You envy her."

"What? What are you—"

"That's why you hate her so much. Not because of her boring stories, but because of the love she had. You've never had anything close to that, have you?"

She didn't answer. She didn't need to. The color seeping into her cheeks was answer enough.

"And even though she lost that love, you still envy her. Because deep down, you don't believe you will ever have something like that. And you know what?"

I could see her throat work as she swallowed. The redness in her cheeks deepened. The glare she was giving me was so sharp it could have cut glass.

Rising to my feet, I looked down at her. "I think you're right. I think a person like you could never have a love so deep."

In the silence that followed, I could hear the sound of a car engine idling at the curb three stories below and the burble of a radio from an apartment nearby.

Dorit Henkin's eyes began to well up. Her chin trembled. She seemed to shrink a little into herself. An uncomfortable truth can bring with it a good deal of pain.

I started for the door, then paused and turned to face her. "Just so you know, David Lipkind still loves Clara. And he has not broken his vow."

And with that half-truth, I let myself out.

11

Hilda Lipkind, fair skinned to begin with, now looked as white as chalk.

We were once again in her living room, and I had just told her the uncomfortable truth she had hired me to uncover. A truth more troubling than what she had originally feared.

"I don't believe it," she said.

I didn't say anything.

"I don't believe it," she repeated, but the tremor in her voice belied her words. A tear trickled out of her left eye and began its meandering path down her cheek. "Why didn't he tell me about her? It's not as though I believed he had been with no woman before me."

"I think he was ashamed," I said. "Because of the vow he'd made. A vow he broke to be with you. Because he fell in love with you. And when she had the accident, it was too late to come clean."

"So he lied."

"Yes."

She nibbled on her lower lip and again clutched at the comforting mirage of denial. "Are you absolutely sure that what you told me is really the truth, Mr. Lapid? From what I understand, there is no actual proof."

"You're right. There isn't. There's only what Dorit Henkin told me. But I believe it to be true, Mrs. Lipkind. Everything makes sense that way."

For a moment, she was utterly still. Then the tears came in earnest. She covered her eyes with her right hand. Her left remained clasped to her ballooning belly. Her shoulders shook with each strangely silent sob.

I let her cry. I could have tried to comfort her, but I was never good at such things. And what could I say?

After a couple of minutes, her crying began to subside. She lowered her hand, unveiling a pair of haunted eyes.

"What does it mean, Mr. Lapid?"

"Mean?"

"That my husband's wife is in reality still alive? Is he really my husband? He's not, is he? Our marriage is null and void, isn't it?"

"I'm not sure what it means, Mrs. Lipkind," I lied, for I was pretty sure she was right.

"And my baby? What does this mean for my baby? Will my baby be considered a—what is it called?—a *Mamzer*?"

"I don't think so," I said, and cursed myself for the faint note of hesitation I heard in my voice.

"But you're not sure."

"I don't think that's the case, Mrs. Lipkind. I'm almost positive it isn't."

I could tell that did little to assuage her fear. She was frantic with worry, and her mind was uncontrollably hopping from one frightening scenario to another.

"Mrs. Lipkind," I said, hoping to calm her down, "no one in authority knows about this. As far as everyone is concerned, you and David are husband and wife."

"You know."

"I do. But I have no intention or desire to complicate matters for you. I am not about to inform on you. You can rely on that."

She gave a short nod of thanks and examined her hands. For a second or two, it appeared that her internal storm had abated. Then her head jerked up and her eyes locked on mine, round and huge. "But she knows. Clara."

"She may never wake up. Chances are she will not recover."

"How do you know this?"

"Her doctor told me."

"But he can't say for sure."

"No. But that's what he believes will happen. Usually, there is no coming back from this sort of injury."

I studied her face as she processed this. The muscles in her cheeks spasmed.

"Mrs. Lipkind," I continued, "even if she does wake up, it doesn't mean you'll lose your husband. The way he feels about you hasn't changed. And soon you will have a child together."

She took a few seconds to consider this. Then she gave a couple of nods—the first tentative, the second assured—and dried her eyes. "You're right. I know you're right. David loves me. I know he loves me. And he will love our baby. He won't leave."

She smiled. A small smile, nothing that would have passed muster with a photographer, but it gave me a sense of profound relief all the same. I had worried about her. Worried that she might crumble under the weight of the truth I had told her. But she seemed okay now, in control.

"Are you all right, Mrs. Lipkind?"

"Yes, Mr. Lapid," she said, and I was glad to hear how steady her voice was. "I'm fine."

"Can I do anything more for you?"

"No. Thank you so much for your work and your concern."

I nodded. "I'll be off now, then."

After I closed the apartment door behind me, I said, "It appears that I brought you here for nothing."

Greta, who had been leaning against the staircase railing, said, "She's okay?"

I looked at the closed door for a moment, getting the urge to go back inside and make sure. "Yes. I think she is." I turned back to Greta. "Thank you for taking the time to come here. I wasn't sure how she would take this."

"You men always expect us women to fall apart at the smallest problem. Some day you'll realize we're much stronger than you think. We have to put up with the lot of you, for one thing." She smiled her kindly smile, the one that made you feel instantly better no matter what sort of day you had. "It was no trouble, Adam. I'm glad I came here."

"Glad? Why?"

"Because it helped you. Earlier today, when you told me about having to come here and tell her what you discovered, I could see how worried you were. About her and about her baby. It feels good to know that I helped."

I smiled back at her. "How about I buy you a cup of coffee as a thank-you? I know a great place on Allenby Street."

She gave me a look. "Do I, by any chance, own this place?"

"It just so happens that you do."

"Your generosity knows no bounds, Adam. Let's go. The sooner we get there, the sooner I can pour us both a cup."

12

Three days later, I was in Nahalat Yitzhak Cemetery. I go there every few months to lay flowers on and say *Kaddish* over the graves of a woman and a child, neither of whom I had ever met.

I was on my way to the exit when I spotted a familiar figure.

David Lipkind.

He was walking down a parallel path toward the gate, his hands once again shoved in his pockets.

I stopped, wondering what he was doing there. I watched as he came across an elderly couple shuffling in the opposite direction. He stepped aside to let them through, and for a split second his eyes roved my way. He showed no sign of having registered my presence. Once the couple had passed, he resumed his brisk walk down the path.

I eyed him until he went through the gate and out onto the street. Then I turned to look in the direction from which he had come. A moment later I saw another familiar figure approaching —this one tall and spare and bald.

Dr. Meles.

He was wiping his glasses as he walked, so he did not notice me until he was right on top of me and I said his name. He stopped short with a start, stuck his glasses on his nose, and peered through them at me.

"Mr. Lapid, isn't it?"

"You have a good memory, Doctor."

"It's one of the prerequisites of my profession. All those Latin names and medicines. You won't find a good doctor with a bad memory. What are you doing here?"

"Visiting a couple of graves. And you?"

Dr. Meles sighed, shaking his head. "She's gone, I'm afraid."

"Clara Lipkind?"

"Yes."

"When did it happen?"

"Last night."

"I'm sorry to hear that. I'm surprised to see you here. Do you usually come to your patients' funerals?"

"No, I don't. I made an exception in this case because it was my impression she had very few friends and so little family."

"Just her brother."

"Yes," Dr. Meles said, his eyes breaking contact with mine. He shifted his feet, suddenly looking very uncomfortable. My antennae went up.

"At what time did she die?"

He frowned at me. "Why do you need to know?"

"I was just wondering if her brother was with her when it happened."

His mouth twitched. "He was not, if you must know. A nurse doing the midnight rounds was the one who discovered her dead."

So you don't know the time of her death, I thought. *Only that it happened before midnight.*

"Do you know how she died?"

"Why are you asking all these questions? For what purpose?"

"Do you or don't you?"

"What does it matter? She's dead." He had raised his voice, and in the near perfect stillness of the cemetery, it sounded loud and shrill. A few heads turned our way. Disapproving glances were shot at us. Dr. Meles's cheeks turned pink.

There was something he wasn't telling me. I decided to press him. "Did she just succumb to her wounds, or was there another cause?"

He gave me a hard stare. When he spoke, his inflection was crisp and formal. "Inform your employer that Clara Lipkind died in her sleep as a result of the injuries she'd sustained in a car accident. That is what the death certificate will say as well. I assume that settles the matter of her policy. Good day to you, Mr. Lapid. I see no reason for us to discuss this any further."

With that he turned on his heel and ventured deeper into the cemetery. I watched him until he stopped before a grave a dozen or so rows away and stood there with his head inclined.

I could have pushed him some more, but I doubted I would have gotten anything else out of him. And what I had gotten was nothing more than a feeling, an intuition, a niggling at the back of my mind.

But perhaps Dr. Meles was right. Perhaps it didn't really matter.

13

I was a block from the cemetery when I heard the rapid scuffing of running feet at my back. I began to swivel, but I was too late. The fist landed squarely on my kidney, sending a jolt of white-hot pain through my body and pushing the air out of my lungs. I stumbled forward, trying to keep from falling, but a foot snaked between my legs and tripped me.

Tumbling onto the sidewalk, I managed to break my fall with one hand. The stone scraped a strip of skin off my palm. It stung like hell. I rolled onto my back as a kick jabbed into me just about where the fist had landed.

I folded in half and retched, acid in my mouth. My vision swam. I heard an angry male voice ask, "Who are you? Why are you following me?"

There was a man standing over me, his fists balled. As my vision began to clear, I could see who it was.

David Lipkind. And he looked as angry as a man could be.

"I don't know what you're talking about," I rasped.

"Don't give me that. I saw you at the hospital and later at the café. And a nurse told me you've been sniffing around asking questions about me, about my—about my sister."

Good ol' Nurse Golobinksi. I should have known she'd talk.

"You've got the wrong guy."

"Like hell I do. I remember your face. And now you trail me to the cemetery."

I raised myself on one elbow and was about to push myself up, but stopped when he growled at me not to move. "I wasn't following you," I said. "I had my own business there."

"You're lying."

I shrugged as best I could given my position. "I'm going to stand up now," I said, and started to do just that.

When he kicked me again, I was ready. Or at least I thought I was. When his foot came streaking toward my torso, I half rolled and tried to loop my arm around his leg as it passed inches from my skin. I succeeded, but it didn't do me much good. Before I had the chance to topple him to the ground, he brought his captured foot down hard on my thigh. I yelled, and my grip slackened. He pulled his liberated foot back and delivered the kick he'd been planning beforehand, right about where an Egyptian bullet in the War of Independence had left a scar on my belly.

I lay there, gasping for breath, the dry scent of street dust heavy in my nostrils. One hand clutched my thigh, the other my belly. He crouched down beside me. When he spoke next, it was through gritted teeth.

"Lie still or God help me..."

Instead of completing his threat, he started poking through my pockets. He flipped through my notebook and tossed it aside. The same fate awaited my lighter and cigarettes. When he got to my wallet, he read my name aloud from my identification card.

"Who the hell are you, Adam Lapid? I want to know why you're following me around."

I hadn't the breath to reply, not that he waited for my answer.

His fingers slid into another pocket and emerged with a folded piece of paper. It was only when I saw his reaction as he read it that I realized what it was. The note Hilda Lipkind had written to me, the one that got me started on this case.

When David Lipkind read it, his mouth dropped open and the anger that had made his face rigid gave way to shock. He had been crouching beside me, but now he plopped down on his backside, clutching the note in both hands, his eyes glued to it.

I took the opportunity to gingerly push myself up to a sitting position. I hurt in multiple places, and I would probably piss blood for a few days, but I did not think I was seriously injured. I watched him as I gathered my breath. He looked like a man whose life had been turned upside down and then rattled around some for good measure.

Finally, he lowered the note. "How much does she know?"

"Everything."

His shoulders sagged. "I should have told her when we first met."

I said nothing. He was right, of course, but he already knew that. He didn't need any input from me.

"I was a fool," he said softly, and it seemed he was talking to himself alone.

"Did you kill her?" I asked. "Did you kill Clara?"

He gave me a dazed look, as though I had spoken in some alien tongue.

"Dr. Meles seems to think you did. So did you kill her, David? Did you kill your wife?"

He slowly opened his mouth, perhaps to answer, when a shout sounded from up the street. It was Dr. Meles, and he was running ungainly toward us. David Lipkind blinked, snapped back into the present moment, saw the doctor approaching, jumped to his feet, and began running away as though pursued by the devil himself.

I couldn't chase him even if I'd wanted to. Instead, I sat there on the sidewalk until Dr. Meles got to me. He was gasping for breath and sweating pretty heavily considering the short distance he'd run.

"What happened? Are you all right, Mr. Lapid?"

He gathered my things, helped me to my feet, and walked me to a nearby bench. He shook his head at the sight of the cut on my hand. "I'm sorry, but I don't have any bandages or disinfectant on me."

"That's all right. I'll clean it up when I get home."

"Make sure you do. It's not deep, but it can still get infected. Any other injuries?"

I told him, and he began probing me with his long nimble fingers.

Before he finished, I asked, "You think he killed her, don't you?"

He paused, his eyes blinking rapidly behind his glasses. "Please, I—"

"Come on. I can see it in your eyes. You don't think she died naturally, do you?"

He wet his lips, hesitating. "I'm not sure."

"Why? Were there signs of foul play?"

"Nothing definite. Some discoloration on the face, that's all."

"The kind that's indicative of asphyxiation?"

He shrugged, his shoulders rising close to his ears. "Could be, yes. As I said, it's nothing definite. Nothing I can be sure of. What he did—if he did it—was likely an act of great mercy. Even if she did one day emerge from her coma, she would likely have suffered from brain damage. She would not have been the same woman she was before the accident."

You don't know that, I almost told him. *You're probably right, but you don't know it.*

"Anyway, it's done. She's buried. And you and I never had this conversation."

He was right. It was over. "Thank you for your help, Dr. Meles."

I began limping away, but stopped when he spoke again.

"If it makes any difference, he's already been punished for what he did—if, indeed, he did do it."

"What do you mean?"

"His wife had a miscarriage. I was there when it happened. It was a boy. Perfectly formed, but too small to survive. Can you imagine, losing a sister and a son in the space of mere hours?"

I lowered my head and drew in a deep breath and let it out slowly. Poor Hilda Lipkind. Her body had failed her again. Then I registered fully what the doctor had said.

"She miscarried in the hospital?"

"Well, it began while she was on a bus. The driver brought her straight to the hospital."

"And it happened the same day Clara Lipkind died?"

"That same night. I have never seen a man as broken as Mr. Lipkind was when he heard the news."

I could well imagine it. Now that I understood everything, I could imagine it very well indeed.

14

I went to see her the next day.

They'd put her in a room on the opposite side of the hall from where her predecessor had lain. I found her in bed, her head turned toward the window, where sunlight slanted in, painting the floor tiles a glowing yellow. She heard my steps and swiveled her head to face me.

My breath caught in my throat at the sight of her. Her belly was not the only part that had shrunk since we'd last met. Her cheeks, her jaw, and her shoulders also appeared to have contracted. Her eyes looked sunken. Ten years or more had been added to her face.

"I heard the sad news, Mrs. Lipkind," I said. "I'm very sorry for your loss."

Her eyes glittered. Her hair looked dry and lifeless, spread over the pillow. In a voice devoid of life and vibrancy, she said, "Thank you, Mr. Lapid. That's very kind of you."

I looked around the room. There were no flowers. No sign that anyone had visited her.

"Where is your husband?"

"Gone."

"Gone?"

"Yes. He came to see me yesterday, told me he was leaving, said that he knew I had hired you."

"I should have discarded your note. I wish to God I had."

"Don't feel bad, Mr. Lapid. None of this is your fault. This is all my doing."

I drew a chair close to her bed. "Where did David go?"

"Away. He wouldn't say where. He told me he had packed his things and left the apartment. He said he knew what I did. Do you know what I did, Mr. Lapid?"

"Yes."

"Did you tell him?"

"No. He mostly figured it out on his own, same way I did. Once I learned you'd had a miscarriage the same night Clara died, and that it hadn't happened in your apartment, I knew you'd killed her. I could think of no other reason for you to risk your child by venturing out."

"You think I'm a monster?"

"No," I said truthfully.

"I just couldn't bear the thought that she would wake up, that I would lose David. I said to myself that it wouldn't really be murder. She's already half in the grave, all I need to do is give her a little nudge. It would be for the best. For my sake, and for David's, and for our child."

Her voice cracked and she began to sob. Her tears came in two thick streams that were pulled down by gravity to her ears and then to the bedsheets. She cried for several minutes. I did not intrude on her weeping. I masked my own emotions as best I could. Guilt was the most prominent of them. If I had not taken this case, Hilda Lipkind would not have miscarried. And Clara Lipkind might still be alive.

"Do you understand why I did it?" she asked, once her crying had ceased.

"Yes. Yes, I do."

Suddenly she reached out and clasped my hand. Her grip was surprisingly strong. "Find him for me, Mr. Lapid. Find my David. Tell him...tell him that I want him to come back to me."

I shook my head. "No, Mrs. Lipkind. I won't do that."

"Why not? I'll pay you."

"Because I don't search for people who aren't in trouble and don't wish to be found. Your husband doesn't wish for you to know where he is. I see no reason not to respect that."

I pulled my hand from under hers and stood to leave.

"Will you tell the police about me?" she asked.

"No. If you wish to confess, that is your business. As far as I'm concerned, you've already received your punishment. Good day, Mrs. Lipkind."

15

Later that night, after closing time, I sat with Greta at my usual table. A pot of coffee stood between us. The cup at her elbow whispered silver wisps of steam. Mine was already empty. I poured myself a fresh cup.

"And that's how it ended," I said.

I had told her the whole story from start to finish, and she had listened with her customary attentiveness. Now she shook her large head, her salt-and-pepper curls bouncing about.

"It's so sad," she said. "And so pointless. If she had only waited, everything would have turned out right for her. Clara would have likely passed away, and David would have been hers and hers alone once more."

"But she couldn't know that for sure. And she must have felt intense fear that any second now, Clara would open her eyes and reclaim her husband."

"So she killed her."

"Yes. But it took her a few days from the moment I told her who Clara really was to build up to it. Hilda Lipkind is not a natural killer. This did not come easy for her. The pressure she felt must have been unbearable."

I took a sip of coffee. Its heat was comforting, and its taste was as rich and wonderful as Greta always made it.

Greta gave me a concerned look. "You don't feel responsible, do you, Adam? Because you're not."

"I know. I just did my job. But I can't help but think that a more perceptive man would have seen some sign of what Hilda Lipkind was about to do, of what she was capable of doing. I saw none."

"Perhaps there was none to see. Perhaps, as you say, it took her a while to get to that point."

"Perhaps," I allowed, knowing that I was inclined to believe this simply because I wanted it to be true. "Yes, you're probably right."

Greta's eyes stayed on my face, trying to gauge my frame of mind.

I smiled. "I'll be all right, Greta. Don't you worry about me."

We both drank from our cups. Smacking her lips, Greta said, "Do you think he'll ever come back to her?"

I had been pondering that same question from the moment I'd stepped out of Hilda Lipkind's hospital room. "I don't know. He might in time. If he ever manages to forgive."

"Forgive Hilda for killing Clara?"

"No. Forgive himself for breaking his vow to Clara."

Greta and I both fell silent. My eyes went to the window and to Allenby Street beyond. Couples strolled by, arms linked. I wondered how many of them were capable of killing for love.

It was a disturbing thought. One I wished to banish from my mind. I took another sip of coffee, closed my eyes, and rolled the warm liquid around my mouth.

Ah, Greta's coffee. It never failed to make me feel a little bit better.

Thank you for reading The Unlucky Woman!

Want a free short story by Jonathan Dunsky?

Join Jonathan Dunsky's readers' newsletter and get a free copy of The Favor.

Go to JonathanDunsky.com/free to claim your copy.

Looking for a great read while I write the next Adam Lapid mystery?

Click here now to read The Payback Girl, a standalone thriller by Jonathan Dunsky!

Please review this book!

Reviews help both readers and authors. If you enjoyed The Unlucky Woman, please leave a review on Amazon. I would greatly appreciate it.

Click here now to leave a review for The Unlucky Woman!

Turn the page for a personal message from the author

AFTERWORD

Dear reader,

Thank you for reading *The Unlucky Woman*. I hope that you enjoyed it. If you did, I'd be grateful if you'd take the time to leave a review wherever you buy or review books. Thank you. I appreciate it.

So far there have been six novels featuring Adam Lapid. This is the first short story in which he features. I wrote it because I love short stories, and I wanted to see how well Adam would play in one. I like the result very much, and I think I'll try to write some more short stories with him in the very near future.

Another reason I wrote it is that many readers, having gotten to the fourth novel in the series, wrote to me asking when the next book will come out. I'm not a particularly fast writer, and I knew it would take me a while to finish a whole novel, so I decided to write something shorter so my faithful readers will know I take their wishes very seriously indeed and do my best to fulfill them.

I hope to meet you again in one of my other books and stories.

Thank you and have a great day,

Jonathan Dunsky

P.S. You can contact me at contact@JonathanDunsky.com with any questions and feedback or connect with me and other readers on Facebook at http://Facebook.com/JonathanDunskyBooks

ABOUT THE AUTHOR

Jonathan Dunsky lives in Israel with his wife and two sons. He enjoys reading, writing, and goofing around with his kids. He began writing in his teens, then took a break for close to twenty years, during which he worked an assortment of jobs. He is the author of the Adam Lapid Mysteries series and the standalone thriller The Payback Girl.

Printed in Great Britain
by Amazon

47040761R00040